Time to Go to Nursery

Penny Tassoni

Illustrated by Mel Four

FEATHERSTONE

LONDON OXFORD NEW YORK NEW DELHI SYDNEY

And adults too!

Who's having fun here?

There are things to do indoors.

What do you like doing?

There are
things to
do outdoors.

What are
the children
doing here?

You can learn things too.

What's going on today?

At nursery there's a time to tidy up.

How many bricks can you see?

BRICKS

Where do they go?

At lunch time you eat
with other children.

Some foods may be new to you.

Which foods do you like?

Some children nap at nursery.

How many children are sleeping today?

At nursery children listen to stories.

And sing...

and dance.

What songs do you know?

Starting nursery
may seem scary
but someone will
always be there...

To show you things.

To help you.

And to give
you a big hug
when you need one.

So wave
goodbye

and go and play.

And then you'll soon find...

It's home time!

Notes for parents and carers

Starting nursery or pre-school is a big step for children but also for parents. Nurseries and pre-schools should have a 'key person' system in place. This means that one adult will be your main point of contact and should help your child to settle in. You can talk to the key person about your child - what they like doing, signs that your child shows when they are tired, nervous or need the toilet! To help your child become familiar with the key person and the other children, it is worth going to 'settling in' sessions before your child is due to start.

Here are some other ways to help your child start nursery:

- Help your child practise being without you by leaving them with someone they already know such as a friend or relative for an hour or so.

- Try to arrange a playdate with another family whose child is due to start or who already goes there.

- Encourage your child to show a little independence, e.g. hanging up their coat.

On the day...

- Talk to your child about what you will be doing while they will be at nursery, e.g. working, doing boring tasks!

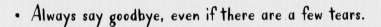

- Allow enough time to get ready for nursery or pre-school. Rushing will increase your child's stress.

- Always say goodbye, even if there are a few tears.

- Refer to a point in their routine when you will be coming back, e.g. after afternoon snack.

- Once you have said goodbye, don't keep popping back. Call the nursery or pre-school if you need to check that your child is fine.

- If you need to go back early because your child is not coping, make it sound to your child as if that was always the plan.

- Avoid using nursery or pre-school as a way of managing behaviour, e.g. don't say to your child 'you won't be able to do that at nursery!'.